CAPTURED BY THE ALIEN

GRACE KENSINGTON

1
───────

The hairs on the back of my neck stood. It happened every time my boss was near. He gave me the creeps and on more than one occasion I had to politely remind him to keep his filthy hands to himself. Ever since I turned down his advances he made up his mind to give me the worst cases and projects. I lifted my tired eyes to see him standing in front of my desk with a smirk. I knew that look. It meant he had something planned—and I wasn't going to like it.

"Ms. Baines, I have a new assignment for you."

Leaning back in my chair I nodded giving him permission to sit in the chair and waited for him to spit it out.

"You're going on a trip."

"Where to?"

"Uoria."

I gulped. Out of all the places he could have sent me and it was to the planet full of the most temperamental species humans had ever studied. "What for?"

"We need to learn more about them, what's in their blood."

I gasped. "You know that's against the rules, Ryan." Everyone knew that the King and Queen made the rules. They still allowed us to do testing, but never of their blood. And I knew what happened to those who tried getting the blood of a Denynso. They never came back that's what.

He shrugged. "You're sneaky enough and no one pays much attention to you. We need to know what makes them so powerful."

His eyes lit up and I shuddered. I knew exactly why he wanted a sample of their blood. It was the same reason every other scientist wanted it, and it was exactly why they had all failed.

"Oh, and preferably the blood from their strongest warrior is what you need to get. You've heard of him, right?"

Of course, I had. Everyone in my line of work had heard of the monstrous Denynso called Pyra. He was one mean son of a bitch and no one wanted near him. Well, besides all the women that vied for a place in his bed. But there was nothing scientific about that.

"You know I won't do that."

He shrugged. "Then your job and reputation are as good as gone. You'll never work again. Not in this field!" He spun on his heel and looked over his shoulder. "Might as well practice saying, "Do you want fries with that?" because that's the only work you'll ever get. You know how much we need this information."

"Wait," I said and sighed. I couldn't lose my job. It was all I had, my livelihood. I'd have to find a way to convince the leaders to let me have a sample and test it. Maybe fudge the results or something. I would find a way. "I'll do it!" I prayed I lived long enough to explain why I was asking for the one thing they'd refused since we learned of their species.

His smile widened as if he had won the biggest prize. He knew I wouldn't be coming back and that was his plan all along. They'd kill me before I got close enough to the warrior, and if I managed to sneak by, he'd break my neck with two fingers. I shuddered. This wasn't going to be a fun vacation. I needed to form a plan and offer the Denynso something they couldn't resist, but I didn't have anything—not really. I only hoped I could get them on the off chance that they wouldn't want me to lose my job. Maybe they'd feel sorry for me, throw me a bone or something. No matter how small it was, I'd take it.

"Good, I knew you'd see it my way. You need to be ready at four a.m."

Then he left me stewing knowing he'd given me an impossible task. If I was going down, I was taking that piece of shit down with me. I smiled evilly. They were an angry species. It shouldn't be too hard to piss them off and let them know it was all Ryan's idea.

After he left me alone, I did what I was best at. I hacked the system and copied the surveillance from my office. Right there I'd be able to prove what was going on to the Denynso, if I could play it. I already knew there wasn't electricity, but I'd charge my laptop for that purpose alone. Proof my boss was a scumbag and it was his idea to send me there to specifically break their rules. Maybe I'd have a chance to survive my stay there, but coming back home wouldn't be so great.

2

———

I was ready to go and waited for my boss well before four. I hadn't slept at all. All night I planned how I would handle the situation my boss had put me in. I knew they would be expecting another scientist. I'd have to meet with them before I step foot on their compound. From what I had learned it was a very secure planet. Warriors scoured the land to keep watch over the humans, and were on the lookout for an attack from their enemies.

I shuddered and thought about what I'd heard about their enemies. There were several horror stories of the attacks on Uoria. The Klimnu were disgusting beasts. Luckily, they hadn't managed to make it to Earth yet or humans would be in big trouble.

Ryan strolled up to me at four on the dot and smiled handing over my paperwork.

"Here's all the stuff you'll need when you get there. I have you down as routine testing for plant and animal life. You're there for up to six months. That should be plenty of time to get what I need." He gave me a look and I didn't miss the tone.

I nodded, but inside I was fuming. He was trying to get me killed. I was his competition, and the one that turned his ass down. He didn't take rejection well, and now I was paying for it. But I was smarter than him and would come out on top.

"All right, well you know how to get in contact if you need anything, but I'm sure you won't."

I kept my mouth shut because this was all a fucking set up. I couldn't believe he'd stoop so low, but maybe it had something to do with the fact that I was up for the promotion he wanted. Luckily, I'd learned to control my Irish temper. My mother always told me one day it would come in handy to have self-control, and now I was learning.

Without a word, I picked up my bags and boarded the ship. I was nervous as hell. This was the first time I was traveling to another planet, and I wasn't too sure about it. I wasn't the type of person who wanted to experience new things. I'd much rather stay in the lab by myself. I felt Ryan's eyes burning into my back and straightened without turning back. He wouldn't get a rise out of me. As soon as the metal door clanged closed I let out the breath I'd been holding and muttered, "stupid ass mother fucker." He would get his.

The very human pilot chuckled. Apparently I spoke a little louder than I thought. Oh well. Everyone knew how I felt about Ryan so it wouldn't be a surprise that I'd be cursing him. They also knew I had a temper and I held a grudge like no other. I glared at the man and he shrugged before getting ready to take off.

The ship shook and my stomach dropped. Leaning back in my seat I held my breath and closed my eyes. My hands gripped the arm rests and I clenched my teeth as I was lifted into the air at an unknown speed. My stomach rose back up into my throat and I nearly lost what little I had eaten. As soon as the ship leveled some I was able to relax but the speed hadn't slowed and I kept my eyes shut hoping the medication I had taken would kick in soon knocking my ass out.

I woke up to the pilot shaking me. I swung my fist and smiled when I heard the satisfying crunch of the bone in his nose breaking. I didn't like being touched especially without permission.

"Shit!" he shrieked. "What the hell, I was only waking you up. I've been trying for nearly an hour. These warriors are starting to get antsy."

I shot up and grimaced. "Sorry," I replied sheepishly. Now I felt bad. "Sorry about your nose."

"It fucking hurts. No wonder everyone is scared of you." His eyes watered and he'd lifted his shirt to catch the blood.

I smirked. "Yeah, well next time refrain from touching me. Use a blow horn if you have to, but keep your damn hands to yourself."

He nodded and winced. "You got it, but please get the hell of my ship."

I stood and stretched knowing I'd just slept for probably five days. My body wasn't ready to stand and I wobbled but caught myself before I fell. "Give me five."

He didn't respond so I took it as an okay and paced the small area while the rest of my body woke up. I needed to be alert when I met the King and Queen. My insides fluttered like butterflies. I wasn't the biggest socialite and meeting people, human or not, wasn't my thing. After the given five minutes I walked behind the pilot and laid a hand on his shoulder. He jumped and looked at me in fear.

"Thank you for the ride, and again, I'm sorry about your nose."

He nodded curtly. The bleeding had stopped but his right eye was almost swollen shut. "I'll remember the blow horn next time."

I chuckled. At least he was able to find humor in getting his ass kicked by a woman.

I stepped off the ship and gasped. It was so familiar, yet not. Everything was so alive. The grass waved in wind, and the sky was almost violet with pinks and oranges. It was breathtaking. I stood taking in the surroundings. The ship rumbled to life vibrating the ground. I didn't even bother looking back. I was stuck here for the next six months. Life was about to get a whole hell of a lot more interesting.

My view was blocked by the largest body I had ever seen. Even I felt tiny compared to the beast in front of me, and instinctively I balled my hands into fists. I had to be in front of the warrior everyone spoke about.

"You're the new one?" he asked in a gruff voice that vibrated along my skin. The sound shot right through my body.

I gulped and looked up, and then up some more before nodding. "Yes, I'm Eden Baines."

He smirked down at me. "Come, you must meet the King and Queen." His voice was a bit tenser, and I wondered why. Must have been that temper I had heard about.

3

———

Pyra wanted to roar. The moment she spoke, something inside of him came to life. As a heat so intense filled him, he was barely able to hold back his gasp. It wasn't acceptable. This measly human was not his mate. She was tiny. There was no way she'd be able to handle all seven feet, and three inches of him.

He wasn't ready to be shackled down by the all-consuming love he'd feel for her. His body was already going through the change, and they hadn't even touched. He'd had this feeling for days. He was edgier than normal, though for him that wasn't saying much. Now he understood why he had flown off the handle more than once and fought five of his brethren.

He stalked to the main house, not looking back. He couldn't look at her, not yet. He wasn't sure he'd be able to keep his hands to himself if he really *saw* her. From what he'd seen she was perfect. Fairly tall for a human woman, pale skin, fiery red hair, that he knew would match the glint in her bright green eyes. He noticed every tiny freckle that dusted her skin. He hadn't missed the slight gap between her two front teeth when she spoke. He also didn't miss the way she averted her eyes or didn't offer her hand like most of the others did. She didn't want to be there, he could tell right off.

She did well to keep up with him. She kept space between them, and it was only her heavy breathing that let him know that his pace was too fast. His mind automatically went to helping his mate and he slowed—too much so, because she slammed right into him and flew back from the force of hitting him.

She yelped and skidded on the soft grass. "Hey fucker," she yelled.

He spun around surprised by the vulgar word coming from her sweet looking lips.

"You nearly killed me!" She stood and wiped her hands on her jeans. Her face was flushed from anger. When she realized all the warriors nearby stopped, her flush deepened and she looked at the ground nibbling her lip.

Pyra wanted to brush her hair from her face, wanted to suck that lip, but instead he bowed his head. "I apologize."

She glared up at him as if she thought he wasn't serious, but she nodded and started walking again. He turned back around and turned toward the path to the Great House.

He could hear the loud thump of her heart but kept his eyes forward. She was a spitfire, but now she was embarrassed. He could sense it. "You know, you sound much like us when we get pissed. You have a formidable temper." he called over his shoulder.

"So I've heard," she grumbled and he chuckled.

"Here that's normal, don't feel embarrassed by your outburst. My brothers were all just surprised to see a human act like us so much."

"I usually have better control."

"I doubt it. I think you react without thinking 90 percent of the time."

"If that was the case I'd have lost my job the first time my boss touched my ass. So no, I think I'm good with control."

He liked her snarky attitude, but what she said pissed him the hell off. He spun and again she ran into him apparently not paying attention and this time before she flew back he gripped her shoulders and held her up. She gasped and looked at him with wide eyes. She felt it too. The touch of the mate, he closed his eyes and bit his lips trying to gain control. All it took was the one touch and he wanted to throw her on the ground and ravage her until she knew who she belonged to. He rubbed his thumbs in circles on each shoulder and then the pain hit.

The little woman brought her knee up a second time when the first wasn't enough. She kneed him hard and shoved him back. Dammit she was tough. He buckled over and groaned. When he lifted his eyes he knew there was fire in them because she backed away fearfully.

"That fuckin' hurt!"

"Well don't touch me asshole!"

Oh yes, she was his. As much as his nuts hurt, his dick was still harder. Her hands were fisted in defense and her chest heaved. More strands of her hair fell from the tie and surrounded her face. Her pouty lips puckered up and her nose scrunched adorably.

When he could stand normally again, because he wasn't lying, it had hurt like a bitch. She was one tough human. "You are amazing," he breathed.

She froze and he could see her body shaking in rage. Someone had hurt her because she learned very quickly that she did *not* like to be touched.

She stood tall and waited, for what he wasn't sure, but he knew she wasn't going to be easy. His mate would challenge him. He smiled thinking his life just got a hell of a lot more interesting. "I won't touch you, but this time I was trying to keep you from getting hurt."

She glared. "Fine, but let's get a move on please. I need to talk to your King and Queen."

"Very well." He wasn't happy that she didn't seem to like him; not even a little bit. He was the type that grew on others over time. Yeah that was it. He led the way and met his parents. They'd heard the commotion and were about to send his brothers for him. He shook his head.

"It's okay she doesn't like being touched." He told them with a shrug. She was behind him so she didn't see the look that passed between him and his parents. His father smirked and his mother, though leery, smiled wide. That was all they needed to know, and no harm would come of her. Ever.

She stood beside him after she had composed herself and gasped. His parents made quite an impression. Father with his foot-tall Mohawk, much like his own, and his pure orange eyes signifying his mating. He was even taller than Pyra at seven and a half feet tall. He had jagged scars from the battles he had survived. They were a badge of honor for their kind. His mother had knee length white hair and her eyes were also orange but lighter. She was tall, thin, and at nearly seven feet her frame was willowy.

"Dr. Baines meet Queen Thiea and King Creia."

She bowed and stepped in front of him. "It's very nice to meet you. Sorry about the—commotion."

His father chuckled. "That's nothing dear. It's common for stifles here. You are Eden correct? I do not like all these—formalities you humans use."

"Yes, I'm Eden."

"Very well, come in dear."

She seemed surprised by how accepting their kind could be. As long as the humans followed their damn rules, and there weren't many. Don't hurt any of them. Don't lie to them, and don't try to steal their blood. Simple, yet so many humans broke those rules. Pyra hoped his human would be the exception. He'd hate to have to protect someone he didn't trust.

4

———————

I followed the King, who looked very much like the warrior following behind me and gasped. No wonder he was so well known. He had a temper, was a cocky son of a bitch, and he was the King and Queen's son. It all made sense now. There was no way in hell I'd get a sample of his blood. Ryan was out of his god damn mind if he thought I'd even try. The man was huge, and I had a feeling it wouldn't be hard for him to snap me in two.

I felt the warrior behind me. My back stayed tense as he stared at me. He kept a good distance between us, but the heat coming from him was outrageous. I looked over my shoulder to see a strange flicker of orange in his eyes. It looked like the King's but it didn't last before they shifted back to blue. I blinked and faced forward so I didn't keep making an ass out of myself. There was something about the giant that brought out the worst in me. I didn't like how my heart raced or my pulse fluttered deep inside.

The King led me into a huge room with a huge table. It was filled with all sorts of food I had never seen before and my stomach dropped. Trying new things wasn't really my thing. I had brought food for myself that would last a year so I wouldn't starve. Pyra seemed to sense my discomfort and he huddled close behind me.

"It's okay. The food is actually a lot better than it looks," he whispered.

He was too close. I could smell his scent. It was a bit spicy and my mouth watered. Suddenly I was hungry for something other than food. "I'm not hungry." I was going to be stubborn as hell. No way would I admit anything going on inside of me right now. I couldn't allow it to happen. It didn't matter that he was the sexiest man I'd ever met, or that I couldn't remember the last time I'd been with a man. No part of his body would touch any part of mine. I was here to study their land. Maybe I would be able to convince myself of that eventually.

He chuckled and I felt his breath whisper across the back of my neck. I clenched my teeth holding back my building anger. Anger was good. I could deal with being pissed. That was normal.

"Please get out of my space," I hissed.

He didn't move back. Instead he placed one of his giant fucking hands on my hip. If I didn't want to look like a complete asshole I had to deal with it, but he would pay. I smiled at the thought of kneeing him in his groin again. This time I wouldn't go easy on him. "If you want to keep that hand, I suggest you remove it from my body," I whispered sweetly.

He leaned into my space even more. Damn he was

arrogant. It didn't seem to matter what the species was, apparently males were all alike.

"Make me.", he taunted. He wanted me to lose my temper. I couldn't—no I wouldn't give him the satisfaction.

"You're gonna regret this, warrior." I officially hated him. I couldn't see why the women all wanted him. Sure, I bet his body was unbelievable, but his attitude sucked. I didn't appreciate men who thought they were god's gift to women. He didn't respect boundaries and that was a big thing for me. I couldn't stand someone who thought they didn't have to stay out of my personal space.

"Oh yeah?" He rubbed his finger across my hip bone, slow and intimate, too intimately. I was going to murder him. "I look forward to anything you dish out, angel."

I chuckled. No one had ever accused me of that before. "We'll see."

Every word that slipped from my lips was met with a touch that threatened to bring me to my knees. I wouldn't let him win. It was physical, that was it.

The King cleared his throat and his smirk in my direction was unsettling. It was as though he was waiting us out.

"Sit please dear."

I gulped and pulled away from the hulking man behind me, but he stepped around me and pulled out the chair. My eyes widened in surprise. I didn't think he had a gentle bone in his body.

He shrugged. "What? My mother raised me too."

I nodded and sat down waiting for the King to tell me the rules. I knew he'd tell me, and I had planned to talk to him about my boss, but I didn't want to do it in front of the warrior.

"I'm sure you know that we are graceful in letting humans invade our lands to run tests, and learn more about our species..."

I nodded.

"There are a few things we do not allow however, and under no circumstances are those rules to be broken. The paper you signed gives us the right to punish you within our laws if you break them in any way."

Again I nodded. I hadn't known that, but then again I should have read the fine print. *If* I made it home I was going to make Ryan sing soprano. He was going to wish he was dead by the time I was done with him.

The King's eyes slanted. "Do you speak, Eden?"

I shrugged. "I'm not much of a talker, or a socialite for that matter. I speak when I have something important to add to the conversation."

"I see," he replied. He was curious about me.

"So, I assume you won't be causing problems. Other than the temper I've already witnessed." With that he smiled.

I blushed. "I do have a temper. Usually it's easier to control."

"Ah, Pyra brings out the worst in you then, or maybe the best yes?"

I laughed I couldn't help it. "I highly doubt my temper is to be considered my best, no offense."

Pyra stiffened and when I glanced at him, he was looking at me strangely. I wasn't sure what he was thinking but he was focused on something. I looked down to see if I had gotten something on my clothes but there wasn't anything there so I shrugged. He was strange. The fact that I was so aware of the giant man sitting silently at the table didn't sit well with me. I didn't like it, not even a little bit.

5

Eden's emotions were so strong that Pyra could nearly taste her nerves. He wasn't sure what triggered it, but he noticed her eyes widened and the scent of her fear coated his skin. He watched her, waiting for another sign as to what could have scared her but she was tough and almost as fast as he felt it, it disappeared. Her posture was still stiff and her jaw was clenched tight.

"Is there anything you would like to ask?" his father asked.

Pyra didn't miss her gaze shift to his uneasily then back to his father.

"I'd like to talk to you," she said and licked her lips. "I'd like for him to leave the room first if you don't mind."

The King's brows rose as did his. He didn't want to be away from her, but at his father's nod he fumed. "Very well," he said to her. He gestured for Pyra to leave. What the hell?

"But—"

His father shook his head warning him with a flare to his orange eyes. "No, it's fine. You may wait for her outside so you can take her to her home while she is here."

He growled and need surged through him. He didn't want her anywhere but with him or with anyone but him. It was outrageous how he was feeling. "Fine," he replied and then he shoved the chair knocking it back. Before leaving he leaned against the back of Eden's chair. His face was right next to hers and he smiled when she shuddered. She wasn't as unaffected as she appeared. "I'll be waiting for you, and then we will talk." It was a promise as much as it was a threat. She'd better not try to sneak off without him.

He could feel her glare. "Don't hold your breath."

He loved her temper. Their relationship was going to be volatile, but for some reason he had a feeling she was going to temper him down. Already he was feeling softer, gentler. He wasn't sure if that was a good thing or not, hopefully it didn't interfere with anything outside of the home. With her he could be different, but with everything else in his life, his temper and rage was a necessity.

He chuckled and took a chance kissing her cheek. He knew she'd hold it together in front of his father. Her body went rigid and he felt her breath stopped for a second before she breathed heavily. Pyra groaned as soon as his lips met her flesh. Her skin was so soft and her scent was so sweet. He couldn't wait to have her. His cock hardened thinking about how soft she'd feel when she submitted to him. He could imagine her sprawled out on his bed and kissed her cheek once more before tearing himself away from her. His eyes shifted to orange and in a rough voice he said, "I'll be outside waiting for you."

She didn't even look at him, but he could feel her rage. She wanted to hit him—badly. He'd be prepared for her anger, but hopefully talking with his father would give her time to cool down. He'd pay for kissing her—twice, but with a smile he realized he didn't care. It was worth it.

He glanced at his father and frowned. His dad was watching her body language. He noticed something Pyra didn't and that meant he needed to talk to his dad.

"Pyra if you would please step out while Eden and I speak, and then and I'd like to have a word with you afterwards." His tone was low and brooked no argument. She wouldn't have noticed the tenseness, but a lump formed in his throat. Something was off with his mate, it was the only explanation.

He nodded and strode outside wondering what his father sensed that he hadn't.

6
———

As soon as the door shut and Pyra was away from me my body relaxed. His touch and taunts were going to drive me mad. I hated them, but worst of all it was because I hated how much I enjoyed his banter, enjoyed his touch. I'd never liked a man's touch before, and that was the worst part of this. My own personal demons would try to suck me in and I'd fall into the nightmare that used to be my life.

Things I hated to think about normally bubbled to the surface, invading all thoughts and feelings, but with him, my past was almost a distant memory. Only my body instinctively reacted as if I was reliving every horrid thing that happened back then. I shuddered. I would never be normal.

"My dear, you look as though you've seen a ghost." He leaned back in his chair and his kind eyes calmed me. There was something about this male that put me at ease. I didn't get it.

"Are you unwell? I know my son can be overwhelming, and I would apologize for his behavior, but I can't because I understand it."

If that wasn't vague or anything.

I didn't understand his son's behavior. It wasn't appropriate, but who was I to tell the King his son needed a lesson in human boundaries. "I'm fine." Leaning forward in my chair and resting my hands on the table I took a deep breath. "My boss sent me here to do the testing."

"Yes, I'm aware of Dr. Austin. I find him to be quite —disturbed."

I chuckled. "That's an understatement, but I'm not here to tell you how much of a creep he is. I need to come clean before you found out somehow—most likely by him."

Now the King straightened in his seat. Not as relaxed as he was. "Come clean? For what?"

I licked my lip and smiled. "He didn't send me here to study plant and animal life."

"Go on."

"He sent me here to try to sneak the blood of your most powerful warrior." I gulped. "I didn't plan to come, and in fact I refused at first, but Ryan hates me. He threatened me so I agreed, but I swear I have no intention of trying to steal any of your blood. I'm an honest person, and I generally don't let others control me, but my work is the only thing I have. If he fired me, I would be ruined. I needed to get him off my back long enough to go over his head. If I get transferred to another company during the time I'm here, then I won't have to worry about him any longer."

The whole time the King watched me as if assessing me for any signs of a lie. "And why would he do such a drastic thing to you, knowing the possibility of you being killed?"

I shuddered. "Two reasons. The first is because I'm up for the same promotion he wants. I'll probably get it because unlike him I have morals and I'm more qualified. And two, he's been trying to get me to date him for years and has sexually harassed me on more than one occasion. I've rejected him more times than I can count."

I hoped that my honesty paid off. I didn't tell people my personal issues, and Ryan's persistence was quite the problem.

"Do you have proof?" I didn't miss the strange look in his eye.

I sighed. "I have surveillance video, but on the video, it shows me agreeing to do it, but I swear I won't go anywhere near your warriors, especially the one Ryan requested the blood from. I'll stick to animals and plants like I originally planned."

He nodded and his frown deepened. "Don't make a promise you can't keep, my dear. Staying away from that particular warrior isn't' going to be an easy task."

"It will if he leaves me alone. If he won't then I promise not to go near him with a needle."

He chuckled and nodded. "Very well, I believe you. I don't sense any lies, but I still want to see this surveillance you speak of. I don't like knowing that someone is actively trying to steal our blood. I think he isn't much of a man to send you to do the dirty work and that angers me very much. We won't be working with this Dr. Austin again. If you're telling the truth, you can stay as long as you'd like to complete your tests of our lands."

I nodded and my shoulders fell. A weight had been lifted. "I need my bag."

"Very well, I will also need my son to see this video. He needs to be briefed in case Dr. Austin sends someone else when he realizes you won't do his dirty work."

I gulped, but shrugged. "Okay my bag is outside."

"Wait here."

I sat back as the King disappeared to get his son. That man was going to be the end of my self-control. I could feel my temper as it mixed with desire. Dammit I needed to cool the hell down, and I certainly didn't need a man to help me in any way.

Pyra came back with the King carrying my bags. He smiled at me, and I nearly lost my breath. It was such an unrefined looked. All of the tough, 'I am man, hear me roar' persona was gone. It was the most real I'd seen him, and I wasn't sure how I felt about seeing his 'human' side. I didn't want to like him. As long as he pissed me off I would be okay.

He handed me my bag and sat in the same chair he had vacated and leaned back in a relaxed position, but I wasn't fooled. He was tensed back like a Cobra waiting to strike. I'd be lying if I didn't find it completely and utterly sexy.

"So, we have a stupid doctor on our hands, yeah?"

The king must have filled him in. I didn't miss the anger in his tone. I knew it was horrible to learn because they'd been working with Ryan for several years now, and I was taking that trust away. I pulled my laptop bag onto the table and slipped my small notebook out. I booted it up and tapped my fingers on the table. "I don't know how well it will work here, or how long my battery will last."

"As long as we see what you told me about."

I looked at him with serious eyes. "You will."

I went back to work and signed in. The file opened easily, and I turned the screen to the king and prayed he would believe me when I told him I had no intention of following through. I really didn't want to endure the kind of punishments they had in mind, and for some reason I really wanted him to trust me, to like me. It wasn't often I cared what someone believed of me, but I found myself caring very much what the King of Uoria thought of me.

The video played and the King watched in fascination as the whole scene played out—just as I had told him.

"What a fucking bastard!"

I jumped when the King slammed his fists on the table and then shoved his chair back. It crashed against the wall and shattered. I had a feeling I was about to see exactly how deadly this species was. He sped from the room, but I barely saw him move. It was unreal. One minute he was there and then poof he was gone. Pyra looked as shocked as I felt.

"Whatever you told him—must have been verified and bad. I haven't seen him this pissed off in ages." Pyra's voice sounded numb to my ears.

"I told the truth before someone else did."

"I'm almost afraid to watch because if he reacted that way, I can't imagine how I'd react."

I sat back and sighed. "Is he coming back?"

"Yes, when he calms down."

I leaned back and closed my eyes wondering if I was going to be punished for my part even though I would never betray them. I'd only be on Uoria for a short time, but I felt— almost at home. When I opened my eyes again he stood there staring at my laptop.

Pyra must not have been able to ignore his curiosity. He stood where his father's chair had been and played the video. The further the video went the more his posture changed, his eyes flared, his body tensed and his jaw was tight. I could hear his teeth grinding together, but he was so calm when he closed the lid to my laptop.

"My father already told me some of why you agreed, but I need to know. I need to hear it from you that you swear you won't try to steal anyone's blood, especially mine."

I gulped. I didn't' get what was so special about their blood but it wasn't my place. I never intended to step where I wasn't allowed. I was a rule follower. "I swear. I only said I would so he wouldn't take my life away from me. Without being a scientist, I'm nothing. It's all I have in the world. I would never break the rules like that, and Ryan knows that, but he didn't expect me to come clean and show you proof of what he is trying to do. He wants me punished."

Pyra's eyes bored into mine. "Why though? Why would he risk your life?"

"He hates me."

"Why?" he asked in a whisper and stepped closer to me.

I could feel his rage, see his body shaking and instead of scaring me, it aroused me. I knew he wouldn't hurt me, but I didn't know why or how I knew it. I just did.

"We are up for the same promotion. He really wants it."

Now he stood in front on me and I looked up. "It's more than that yeah?"

I gulped. "I don't know."

"Don't lie to me; I know what you told my dad."

Of course he told him about the other stuff. I'd hoped he hadn't and now he was testing me. It didn't feel good. "I rejected him."

"Why did you reject him?"

I chuckled. "Because I hate him."

"No other reason?"

"I don't like to be touched, and he has a problem keeping his hands to himself. I've broken his nose and his wrist."

He nodded and moved closer. Our bodies were almost touching, but not quite. I couldn't breathe. His body heat was suffocating. He was a man in every sense of the word, and I was drowning in his want, his need.

"He didn't leave me alone," I whispered.

"I'll kill him."

I gasped and shook my head. "No."

He leaned in and his lips were so close I could taste him. As soon as I shut my eyes and was about to close the distance the king came back in a whoosh and cleared his throat. I jumped back from Pyra and shook my head. I glared at him and he stepped back. I was pissed at myself. I almost caved, and if not for his father I would have felt his lips on mine. I wasn't sure what was worst; the fact that I yearned for the touch and it was interrupted or that he had the balls to try it in the first place.

7

———

The King came back into the room interrupting the almost kiss. I was grateful because I didn't want to cave. No matter how much my body disagreed with my mind. It didn't matter that he was attractive and that there was a huge part of me that wanted to jump him. I didn't know what was going on, but I couldn't allow it to happen. His growl of frustration sent a thrill down my spine.

His father sat back down considerably more calm, but the rage was right below the surface, simmering. "Dear, I wanted to say thank you for coming forth with this video and being honest right away. Not many of you would do that, and I know that I've had to send many humans back home because I'd caught them doing unfavorable things. I wish there were more people like you from your world. After speaking to my wife, we have decided to discuss a compromise. I will get back with you when we decide exactly what it will be. Until then, please explore as much as you'd like, but keep the rules in mind, and do not under any circumstances, contact your boss. If you do, you'll be sent home, and you'll never be allowed to come back."

I sighed in relief. "Thank you for trusting me, and I have no intention of contacting Ryan. I look forward to studying the plant and animal life."

He stared me down with gentle eyes. "I don't know why I trust you, but please don't abuse it. I do hold grudges once the faith is broken."

I held out my hand, the first initiation of physical contact. He looked at my hand then back at my face as he pulled my hand into his. They were warm and soft and instead of shaking it he grasped it between both of his hands. Heat engulfed me and there was a strange zing, almost like magic before a slight bit of pain, and when he pulled back there was a small symbol on my hand. I gasped and studied it. It was small and the black lines swirled and twisted nicely together. It was intricate, but when I looked harder I noticed the lines were letters.

"It's a mark. Letting others know you are one of us now. It's means, 'sister of our brethren' in our language."

I knew they didn't do this often—if at all, and I was honored. Tears filled my eyes and I sniffled. "Thank you. I promise you won't regret it!"

He smiled. "And you don't have to worry about your problem back home anymore."

"I didn't tell you what he did to have you fix it. I was dealing with it."

He rolled his eyes and I swear he looked just like his son. "I know which is why I did it." He smiled and rubbed the mark. "And how exactly have you handled it? By ignoring his advances and threatening him. You're tough, but apparently it didn't work or he wouldn't have sent you here to break our most sacred rule."

I slumped in my seat. "I didn't know what to do."

"You can stay here." Pyra said and I looked at him. I'd forgotten he was even in the room.

"Uh, I don't know if I'd fit in here too well. Besides you never let humans stay for more than six months, though I'll stay the whole allotted time if that's all right. The longer I'm away from home the better right now."

"There are exceptions to every rule," he said but he watched his father as if waiting for him to chime in.

The king nodded and smiled kindly at me. As much as Pyra drove me wild with anger and the harder it was getting to fight his advances, I felt the exact opposite about his father. I felt at ease with him. I'd never had a dad, but if I could imagine one, King Creia would be the perfect image.

"You may stay. When my mate and I decide on what we plan to do we will have lunch, but for now you must get settled. Pyra will take you to your cabin."

I nodded and stood. "Thank you, I'm exhausted." And I was. I'd 'slept' the whole way, but it wasn't really sleeping. I was basically unconscious the whole time.

Pyra stood and walked over to his father. They hugged and I heard faint whispers, but I was too tired to care. I picked up my laptop and slid it back into my bag.

He took the strap from me. "I've got it."

Normally I would have fought him, but every part of me hurt. I don't know why it took so long to kick in, but I wasn't sure if I'd make it much longer before crashing. "Thanks," I muttered.

He nodded and I followed behind him leaving the

house. He jogged down the stairs and I sighed. My legs were heavy, and it felt like I wasn't moving at all. Pyra stopped and studied me.

"I could carry you if you want." I didn't miss the tone. He was messing with me. I thought.

That was all it took to wake my body up enough to get moving. "In your dreams warrior," I sneered at him.

He laughed and spun walking down a path. I followed as fast as I could. I would not give him the satisfaction of knowing I really wanted to drop to the ground and sleep for a week.

8

He'd been so close to tasting those suckable lips, and then his father had to come back and ruin it all. She was so beautiful, perfect really. He loved that she was honest. The video had made him want to rip the man to shreds, but it was what his father had told him about the scumbag that really pushed him over the edge. Sexually harassing his mate, now that was grounds for killing.

There was so much to her. She clearly had a problem with others touching her. He wanted to know what had happened. Why the thought of being touched turned her into a quivering mess or a ball of rage. Something happened to her, but he had no clue what it could have been. Humans were strange creatures. He'd find out everything one way or another.

He turned and saw her standing on the porch. Exhaustion filled her eyes, but she was stubborn and wouldn't admit how tired she was. Not to him at least, but she told his father. Pyra loved it. As soon as it looked like she was done all he had to do was taunt her, and she was back to being the independent woman he was becoming accustomed to. He'd noticed it right from the start.

He shook his head when he saw the mark of his kind on her hand. She was the first in years. He couldn't have been more shocked when his father marked her with their sign. He knew it wasn't because she was his mate. The king wouldn't honor someone with that status if he or she wasn't worthy, and being his mate didn't make her worthy, even if it made her family. She had already earned his respect and that was tough as shit to do.

He led her to the newest cabin. It was the closest to his home. If he had his way she'd be in his home, and in his bed, but he knew that wouldn't happen. Not until he got her to cave. She had to admit that she liked him at least a little bit, and right now by the way he felt her emotions and the fact she was glaring daggers at his back, he knew that wouldn't be happening—today. He couldn't help but laugh. She wasn't going to make it easy and as frustrating as it was not to be able to pull her into his arms anytime he wanted, he was proud to have a mate that didn't cave. He loved a challenge, and he always got what he wanted. And he wanted Eden.

At first, the thought of having a human mate wasn't appealing at all, but the more he was around her the more he wanted her, and it wasn't just physical. That's what shocked him the most. He was a sexual being and proved it time and time again with the females. None of them were anything more than gratification, and they knew that, but with her, he could imagine lying with her, holding her. He shook his head. His brothers would bust his nuts if they knew the soft thoughts running through his head. He never thought he'd be that way, but his father told him it would be the best and worst feeling in the world. Falling in love was everything to his kind.

The path narrowed and dipped deeper behind the trees. She'd have all the privacy she wanted. The cabin was the most updated and he was glad he picked it. She followed behind him breathing heavily.

"We're almost there."

"I'm fine," she replied.

He sped up and jogged up the stairs. Pulling out her key, he unlocked the door and went inside. He put her bags down. He was back outside and sitting on the steps before she made it.

"You could have waited for me."

He shrugged. "You're too slow."

She stomped a foot and cringed. "My legs are shorter than yours, you jerk."

He laughed. She was too tired to put any heat behind her voice. "Uh-huh, has nothing to do with how tired you are?"

She jutted out her lip. "Nope, I'm fine."

"Okay well let's go in. I'll show you around your new home."

Her eyes widened and she licked her lips.

Interesting.

His eyes tracked the movement and he wanted to trace the path her tongue made.

"You don't need to show me around. I'm sure I can figure it out."

His eyes shot back to hers. "You need to know how to work everything. There is no electricity here."

"I know."

"So I'll help you get set up and then I promise I'll leave you alone."

"Fine, let's get it over with." She said and pushed past him to climb the stairs.

He watched the sway of her hips and it took all his will power to keep his hands to himself. He went in behind her and shut the door. He sighed in relief knowing he was alone with her. That's all he wanted. If she would get to know him, the real him, maybe just maybe things would be different and she wouldn't hate him so badly. He hoped she'd throw him a bone. His fingers itched to touch her skin, but he knew that one touch would lead to so much more, and she wouldn't let that happen.

9

The door clicked shut and I froze. I was too tired and that was worrisome. I wasn't sure I'd be able to stop myself from falling into his arms. Not when my body seemed to crave the giant beast. I didn't know what it was about him, but each time he was near me, my heart galloped and my core clenched in need.

I smiled. If it was only physical attraction, if I caved maybe the need would go away? My time here would run smoother if I didn't constantly feel aroused, and from what I'd heard about his reputation, once he got what he wanted he'd leave me alone. It was a win-win, only my heart jumped at the thought of being just another woman he bedded.

I took a deep breath and turned towards him. In the cabin, he was even more imposing. He prowled toward me, with desire in his eyes. "I need to take a shower."

"Water runs well here. I'll wait."

I glared. "Or you can leave and come back after I'm done so I can have some privacy."

"There's a door."

I knew he wouldn't give more than that. "Fine, but stay out of the room."

He held up his hands and smiled wide. "I'll be on my best behavior."

I laughed. "Somehow I don't think I should be reassured by that."

"Guess you'll find out, yeah?" He started down the hall with my bags and I followed behind him. His shirt was so tight I could see each one of his muscles flex with every move he made.

He pushed open the door and placed my bags by a large bed. "This is your room, and the bathroom is right over there. We may not have electricity, but we use solar power to work our heating system. You'll get approximately ten minutes before the water turns cold."

"Okay, thanks." I replied and waited for him to leave. He stood and stared for several seconds. "I think I can take it from here."

"Are you sure? I could help."

He chuckled but it sounded like he was struggling. He wasn't messing with me like he had since I stepped foot on Uoria. I'd have to get better at controlling myself. Or maybe I needed to loosen up. Here was sexy man in my room who obviously wanted me. The lust bubbled over with how he devoured my body. I wanted see how far he'd go.

He stood facing me and I smiled. It was a real smile and I stepped in his direction. He flinched but didn't move back. I shrugged and before he knew it I pulled my shirt off over my head. All thoughts left me. At that moment the only thing that mattered was him touching me.

He groaned and his eyes widened. The orangish color I'd seen a few times was back. I cocked my head to the side watching him, waiting, but he was frozen.

I reached behind my back and undid the clasp to my bra and slid it to the floor. His giant body shook and it looked like he was using every ounce of his self-control to keep his feet planted on the floor. He was surprisingly in control. It was impressive, but I wanted him to break. I wanted to feel the heat I saw behind the depths of his strange colored eyes that did strange things to me. They called to me, said I needed to submit to him. I was his for the taking. Instead of getting pissed I moaned and my eyes fluttered shut long enough to let the feelings of his desire wash over me.

When I opened my eyes, he was still watching me. His chest heaved and his lips parted when I slid my hand underneath the waist band of my jeans. I wiggled my hips and pushed them down my legs taking my panties with them. In a matter of minutes I stood naked in front of a man I really couldn't stand, but one I wanted desperately.

"Oh goddess, you're perfect," he whispered.

I hadn't expected him to say something so perfect and his reverence shot to my core. I nibbled my lip waiting for him to take control, but he was still frozen in his spot.

"Are you going to stand there and stare at me, or are you going to move your ass over here?" My snarky attitude shook him out of his daze and he growled.

He strode to me in two giant steps and crushed my

body to his. His mouth slammed down on mine and I lost my breath. There was so much power behind his kiss, and when his tongue entered my mouth I was done for. I gasped and wrapped my arms around him. He lifted me from the floor and tightened his hold. My body lit on fire.

When he pulled back he was panting for breath. "I thought you didn't like me," he said.

"I don't."

"Sure," he replied with a small smile and kissed me again.

My shower was forgotten when he tossed me on the bed. I watched as his clothes were shredded from his body. The pile on the floor built and then he climbed on the bed hovering over me. I wanted to warn him, but it was too late. He slid into me with a speed unknown to man. I screamed and my muscles clenched. He froze and stared down at me.

"You were an innocent?"

I glared. "Not exactly, but it's been a long time, like years, and that fucking hurt." Tears slid down my cheeks.

"I'm so sorry Eden." And for the first time I saw real regret in his eyes.

My heart clenched I didn't like him upset. "Hey, it's okay, but be gentle with me."

I wasn't sure if he was capable of gentle, but he proved me wrong. He took his time making love to my body. Each thrust was slow and steady. I caught on to his movements and lifted my hips meeting each new thrust. My body stretched and it no longer hurt. It was as if I was made for him. He fit me perfectly and when he twisted his hips the tip of his erection hit with such a force I climaxed without warning. My body bowed and my muscles tensed around him, holding him in place. I felt him come and we stayed locked together until both of our bodies came down from release.

10

———

I lay looking at the ceiling wondering what the hell I just did. My body ached, but mostly I felt more relaxed than I ever had. Pyra was next to me, and even though I could feel his eyes on me I didn't look at him.

"You weren't ready."

My eyes filled with tears. No I most certainly was not ready. No matter how much I enjoyed it at the moment, now—now I felt dirty. I shook my head doing my best to hold the tears back.

"I'm not sorry we made love, but I am sorry it was too soon for you."

I looked at him to see how his eyes glowed orange at me. I don't think they ever turned back to his normal blue since I had stripped. "I need to go for a walk."

He nodded and got out of bed. "I'll go with you."

I rolled out of bed and flinched. "No, I want to go alone."

"Okay, I'll walk you out then at least. I have to go meet

with my brothers. It's time for my scheduled patrol anyway." His voice was low and there was none of his playful banter.

"That's fine, I'll get dressed." I stood and gasped. Every muscle in my body was sore. I knew he hadn't meant to hurt me, but oh how I hurt.

He growled and I looked over at him. He frowned and looked disheartened. "I hurt you."

"I know you didn't on purpose."

"I should have known. It didn't have to be painful for you. If I wasn't such a jack ass you'd be fine right now."

"Hey, didn't I tell you it had been a very long time. That's not your fault."

He turned away and picked up his clothes. They weren't torn at all. He got dressed without looking my way. I dressed in the same clothes I had been wearing and put my shoes on. I needed out. The scent of sex filled the air and it was too much.

Pyra walked in front of me and I followed stiffly behind him. Shutting the door, I took a deep breath of the air. It was clean and fresh, so much better than home. I followed him down the stairs and tipped my head back. The sun was no longer up here, and stars filled the sky. They were huge and so much easier to spot than at home. It was amazing how much Uoria was like home, but it was fresher. The Denynso took care of their lands. They didn't take anything for granted.

Out of nowhere I was lifted in the air and thrown. I screamed and my eyes widened. The thing that threw me sped into my direction and wrapped a clawed hand around my throat stopping me midair. My body jerked forward like whiplash. My heart thudded rapidly in my chest, and I lost my breath.

I'd never seen anything so vile as the creature before me. His eyes were red and his sharp teeth dripped spit. He ran his tongue along the tips and leaned in toward me. I tried to scream again, but I'd lost my voice. Kicking out I landed a blow to his lower body. He roared and dropped me. I fell to the ground with a thud. My back burned and the scent of copper filled my nose. It was blood—and it was mine. The monster rushed down toward me, and even as I tried to lift my hands he fell on top on me holding me down. His claws bit into my wrists.

"You smell sweet." The thing said and then his teeth were in my neck.

My voice was gone. I cried and sobbed, but each move I made only seemed to make the creature more excited. He sucked harder on my neck taking more of my blood. His grunts and groans did nothing to ease my fear. I felt myself fading away. I'd only been on Uoria for a day and I was already going to die. I smiled. At least I'd never have to go back home again.

The thing's body was ripped from mine and I saw orange eyes staring down at me. I lifted my shaky hand up hoping he'd end it for me. Everything hurt, and I didn't want to suffer.

Instead he bent down lifted me carefully into his arms. The feel of his warmth surrounding me was a comforting blanket. He moved so fast, but I was fading faster. There was nothing to do but wait.

TBC

(To be continued in Part II...)